First published in the United States, Great Britain, Canada,
Australia, and New Zealand in 2000 by North-South Books Inc.,
an imprint of NordSüd Verlag AG, CH-8005 Zürich, Switzerland.
First paperback edition published in 2007 by North-South Books Inc.
Distributed in the United States by North-South Books Inc., New York.
Library of Congress Cataloging-in-Publication Data is available.
A CIP catalogue record for this book is available from The British Library.
ISBN: 978-0-7358-1389-2 (library edition) 10 9 8 7 6 5 4 3 2 1
ISBN: 978-0-7358-2146-0 (paperback edition) 10 9 8 7 6 5 4 3 2
Printed in USA by CG Book Printing, North Mankato, MN 56003, January 2010.

www.northsouth.com

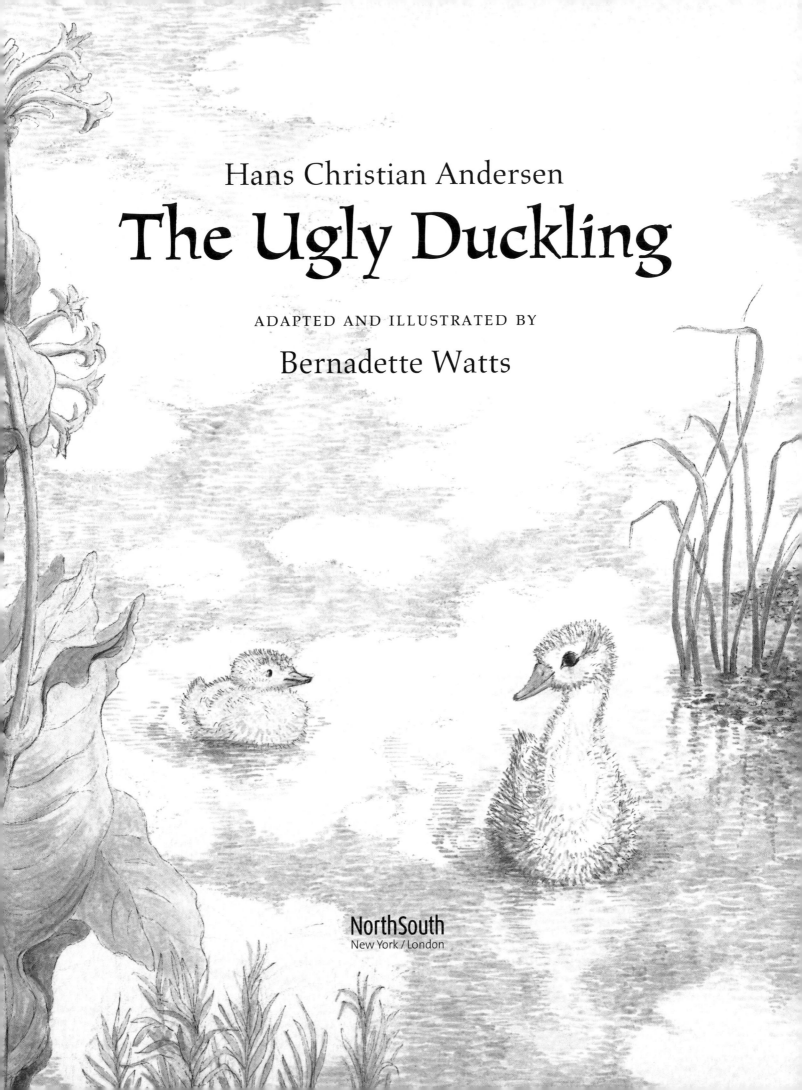

Hans Christian Andersen

The Ugly Duckling

ADAPTED AND ILLUSTRATED BY

Bernadette Watts

NorthSouth
New York / London

It was a beautiful summer day. The sun was shining down on an old house surrounded by a moat. Bushes, reeds, and flowers grew by the water's edge. In the shade of some big leaves, a duck was sitting on her nest, waiting for her eggs to hatch. It was taking a very long time, but finally, one after another, the eggs cracked and out came the ducklings.

 Only the biggest egg still lay there. The mother duck settled down again and waited for it to hatch.

At last the big egg cracked open. The mother duck looked at the new duckling and thought: How big and ugly he is! He doesn't look like any of the others. Perhaps he is a turkey chick and is afraid of water. I'll take him to the moat to see if he can swim.

The mother duck and her ducklings jumped right into the water. One duckling after another followed her—even the ugly duckling jumped in eagerly.

"So he isn't a turkey chick after all!" said the mother duck, relieved. "It is my own child. Actually, now that I look at him again, he isn't ugly at all." Feeling contented, she led her ducklings to a farm nearby.

But when they reached the farmyard, the other birds began to ridicule the ugly duckling. They pushed him, pecked him, and chased him around the farmyard.

Even the duckling's brothers and sisters were unkind to him. Finally, the mother duck cried, "Oh, if only you were far away from here!"

So the ugly duckling ran away. He flapped over the fence, startling all the birds in the bushes who then flew off. That is because I am so ugly, thought the duckling. He ran on until he reached the wide marsh where the wild ducks lived. There he lay, trembling the whole night long. At sunrise the wild ducks found him. "How ugly you are!" they quacked. "But we don't care as long as you stay out of our way."

The duckling was lonely and frightened in the marsh. After a few days, a fearsome dog appeared and bounded up to the duckling. The duckling was terrified! But the dog turned around and ran off without harming him. How lucky! thought the duckling. I look so ugly that even a dog doesn't want to eat me!

The duckling rushed away across the marsh as fast as he could.
At the edge of the marsh, he came to a tumbledown cottage.

The duckling slipped through a crack in the door. There he saw an old woman sitting by the fire with her cat and her hen. They allowed the duckling to stay for a while, but only at the back of the room.

"Now I will get some duck eggs!" said the old woman.

But the duckling didn't lay any eggs. He sat sadly in the corner and dreamed of warm sunshine and swimming. Shunned by the cat and the hen, he went out into the world once more.

Eventually he came to a lake where he could swim and dive. One autumn evening, just as the sun was setting, a beautiful group of birds flew by. They were dazzling white with long necks. They were swans, although the duckling didn't know that, and they thrilled him. He had never seen such beautiful birds.

Winter came and it was bitterly cold. It would be very sad to describe all the misery the duckling suffered that long, harsh winter.

Then one day the warm sun shone again. It was spring. The duckling spread his wings and flew away from the dikes and the marshes and came to a lake. There he saw three swans gliding majestically over the water. "I will fly to those beautiful birds!" he said. "They may peck me to death because I am so ugly, but it doesn't matter." So the duckling glided down onto the water and swam toward the swans.

The duckling bowed his head over
the water, expecting to be killed.
But what did he see in the water?
He saw his own reflection, no longer an ugly
duckling but a beautiful swan! The other swans
swam round him and stroked him lovingly
with their beaks.

What does it matter where one is born if one has been hatched from a swan's egg?

He remembered all the pain and misery he had suffered, but now everything had changed. He raised his long, slender neck and trumpeted: "I never dreamed of so much happiness when I was a wretched ugly duckling!"